Welcome To Zone X

By

George A. Hart

George A. Hart / Rev. Caesar 999

ISBN: 978-0-9840313-8-2

Welcome to Zone X

Title Page 1

After centuries of destruction,

Man lives in total chaos.

From flesh to metal they survived eternity.

Upon eternal madness they see no reality.

Lost in hell alone they seek peace.

Forced forever into war by the controllers.

Never to reveal true face and honor new codes.

They see no end to their despair and torture of all their lives.

Seeing never again the light beyond.

Caught evermore into the wasteland they created.

By living in separate unions upon earth.

Thinking back if they chose another way of life.

The world they lived divided.

If only they decided living as one.

And now they fight endless battles leading all to death.

So, they said in their time with a laughing cry.

Welcome to Zone X!

Welcome to Zone X

Title Page 2

Here in the new world of total law,

And justice the new way.

The world in the year 39.5 – A. L. After Life.

This underworld of chaos is bound to destruction.

The earth wars destroyed all known cities.

What was left of man is now lifeless machines.

Machines of great power and control.

For they are the controllers.

Now, still thousands of years later.

The rebels still build their numbers.

As the hunters search for the survivors.

To the great wars of earth, now known as the wasteland.

They are the rebel leaders.

They've survived because no man is flesh no more.

For they are interfaced to machines.

They are living metal.

When captured they're never seen again.

They are sent to the heart of Zone X.

And there they are transformed to X Men,

The Enemy Soldier.

Chapter 1. The Forging

The controllers reign started after the earth,

Became the wasteland and all became hell.

The surviving engineers forged the Life-force Matrix.

Its purpose was to remove and separate the human soul from the flesh,

To overcome fear and pain and all other physical or mental torture.

And to survive this world and the worlds to come,

Until its use was needless.

By this you are no longer a man, you are an X Man.

From their cybernetic implants produce a cyborg.

After testing it on mutants that roman the wasteland.

At first it seemed to reanimate life.

Then after many successful alterations,

The Life-Force Matrix contains and consumes the souls.

The completed cyborgs showed signs of treachery.

Taking only commands from their creator.

Now, known we have no control over them.

They may soon turn on us.

We did not know at the time it was altering itself.

But we did take actions, we ordered it shutdown.

The guards never returned though it's virtually invincible.

And its defenses were superior, the base did have a self-destruct,

Mechanism linked to it.

Never thinking at this time about destroying the base.

Night after night men would disappear from their quarters,

Slowly building Controller numbers.

The engineers had long disappeared by now.

Now, all over the base scenes take place.

Anyone not cooperating with them was taken.

Our leaders too busy to notice while they watched,

Their troops have implants completed.

The volunteers and most critically wounded,

And the insane troops were already sent to be altered,

Right after the mutants without study or research.

Those man are lost eternally and from here on,

They will be known as X Men.

Who have given their lives for our survival.

Now, realizing they have total control of the base,

Attempting to set the self-destruct sequence.

Figuring out that the LFM has reprogrammed the computers.

It's now ordering the capture of all men.

Puzzling them for we too are cyborgs.

But we have individual minds and our souls intact.

Though they have strength and ultimate intellect.

For we have the power to create,

And to the power to destroy.

Time is what we need and time is what we've got.

The base being destroyed from inside out.

They sweep it capturing all without metal.

And fighting those with metal, adapt and overcome.

Is what they did destroying us one by one.

We scatter and through the smoke and fire,

Some of us find the escape ships programmed,

For base 2 and 3, the lunar base and orbital base.

We could not send for help all channels were scrambled.

Being we are on our own until we reach our destinations.

Watching what's left of our base explode into atoms.

As again we are forced to fight.

For we are never free of war if only we became one,

Before it was too late now our race is doomed eternally.

As we raced towards our destinations,

Behind us we seen a dimensional hole.

The light from it would melt your eyes from your face.

If you were flesh but we are metal.

Then from it flashes of light, beams of destruction.

And the source of that hideous crafts of great evil power,

Thrown upon us from behind.

Explosions all around us as our friends lose their lives.

Fire and darkness and death the drip of blood.

Through our metal shields then cold light.

And barren yields all became quiet as they returned,

To the center of what is known as Zone X.

Chapter 2. Fall and Rise

From earth we've risen.

And there we lived what we called life.

Now, again we ask is this reality,

Or but a never ending dream?

Being has this all been dreamed before?

In death we live the new dream,

Or but the true reality again we see.

No truth or proof of our own existence.

In the grounds of eternity and beyond.

From there we thought living death as to life.

In a world of false life to live is to die.

And to die is to live a true life.

Around us we became death and then we lived once again.

Our lives became one and together,

We became all.

Now, upon the lunar base we strengthened our numbers.

In the darkness we pondered within our souls.

There we spotted them a blinding white light.

Then it seemed from nowhere they appeared.

Again we spied them in detail.

From the reflection in our eyes.

At such close distance at which we've never seen.

The most hideous craft our flesh bleeds,

And our metal rusts.

Mounted upon these huge crafts,

Horned beastly skulls.

Protruding through its blaring eye sockets,

A powerful weapon made of light.

Being hurled upon us with great speed.

Thousands of crafts fall toward us.

From space they crash upon this moon.

There we trembled with fear and horror.

For we know death awaits us.

Death as to life their death we face this hour.

Attempted to defend our ground.

They came down with much speed.

We scattered and fought as we pulled back.

Our weapons ran low and our fuel went dry.

The dark space around us was lit,

By total fire power and burning wreckage.

And from these craft came a many.

They pushed us back and back.

With no remorse they slaughtered us.

And these cyborgs are known to be X Men.

Into the base we fled.

With no retreat they swarmed around us.

What power we thought.

Has the Life-Light Force Matrix merged with a mere man?

For he is mortal no more, immortality is immense.

From inside our shields blew out.

For the Hunters are unnoticeable.

They creep in and out without any attention.

While we scramble in our heads.

How will we retaliate against such a force?

Now, with no hope of our escape.

Bombarding their crafts head on into our world.

Impatiently, I alone lead what's left,

Of our mutilated forces.

Deciding to withdraw our attack.

For it did no good, no help at all.

Again we turned to look upon death.

Cornered in we were annihilated one after another.

Then all went dark, I saw nothing,

Heard nothing, I was falling and then light, then dark again.

After what I thought was hours I awoke.

As I lie dying deep in the depths of the lunar base.

Pinned down under tons of rubble, all my implants damaged,

And un-operational, I heard my brothers' war cry of death.

As I wished and begged to god, if there is a god,

That I could die honorable like the others.

As tears of blood flowed from within.

For we are living metal.

Hearing a voice I turned there, I saw an old man,

Upon his knees as he said, take this the Dark Matrix of death.

For death is life all again.

Looking in my hand, seeing the crystal.

He says, now become one and complete your eternal quest.

I looked back and saw nothing but darkness.

As I saw before this vision.

It must have been real, this crystal I hold,

Glows with a dark-light from which I will reveal.

The true life that which we shall live eternal.

By this once again I see beyond.

From here on we are rebels no more.

We will be known as the survivors.

Chapter 3. The Excursion

There now again I awoke.

To say I was in a strange new world.

And much of my memory I've lost.

Watching the chamber seal around me,

From the bottom and from the top.

A cylinder chamber enclosed as I watch,

The light disappear as I glanced out.

And seen another being harnessed into alignment,

As if he is to follow after me.

Though I didn't know what was happening,

A strange voice came aloud.

It said relax and everything will be fine.

A deep feeling inside of me felt something was wrong.

For I've heard that voice before,

An old friend who was captured by The Controller Network.

From the other side I saw a being of great size.

Standing before me linked by mechanical structure,

To the chamber I was sealed into.

Not remembering the Crystalys that I possessed,

Which was captured when I was, when The Lunar Base,

Had happened to fall into enemy hands.

Still not knowing my name I thought it was the end.

For now I knew the Matrix was captured and only I can merge with it.

Our forces almost completely destroyed or captured,

And now I was finally welcomed to Zone X in an altered way.

Being the torture and despair isn't yet to begin.

Now, I was completely sealed into darkness.

Then a magnified light by a thousand times,

Seemed to just glow from nowhere.

A heat at the radius of the sun at total balance,

From one end of the universe to the other end.

With a cross between life and death equally,

Combined into such a small chamber.

But so delicately interwoven it will not,

Harm the bare human skin.

Within seconds I heard a disturbance,

Right outside in the alteration room.

I heard laser weapons firing.

Thinking something was wrong,

And I was about to die again.

As the chamber burst into flames around me,

Crashing out just before it blew I seen,

My fellow survivors struggling to escape.

With single laser bursts from the LFM.

I seen them disintegrated right before me.

Diving into the lift rotary just missing being destroyed.

As it comes to a stop not knowing if it,

Was moving upward or deeper into this strange place.

Now, the door opens and with perfect timing I jumped the two guards.

One mistake can mean my death or capture.

Taking their weapons and suit sending,

Them straight to hell in a flash,

I infiltrated their search party.

By my elite training of infinitely superior,

Mind of the enemy so it won't take them,

Long to realize they just been utterly fooled.

Ultimately, by my superior intellect of the advanced,

Human mind interfaced to machine which doesn't mean,

I'm impregnably immortal though my intelligence exceeds,

Their puny standards I do credit myself for this,

Victory of my self-image for it is not over for us.

Until we bring ourselves to realize we are inferior,

To their logic.

Thinking with all the patrols looking for me,

I thought the inner core chambers.

So, I crawled through a thin passage way,

Until I finally hit the main corridor.

I had to move fast because I knew about the censors,

And they were tracking me. I tried not to activate the,

Inner defenses evading them I came to a door.

The only way to get through was to blast it.

With a quick shot it opened also the alert sounding,

And laser cannons came out of the walls.

They sensed heat so I became the prime target.

Next thing I knew, I was running with laser blasts,

All around me. I saw at the end of the corridor,

The main control for them. Getting braised I ducked,

And rolled out and shot the fuck out of the main controls.

As I stepped into the next chamber I was amazed.

At the immensity of these core duct terminals,

While looking down no bottom could I see.

As they blinked in pattern so I climbed steadily,

Downward as my goal was to find the Matrix,

And escape these premises.

And there I undermined the guards as I entered,

What seemed to be the making of a time displacer

Unit which had been recently used and the date I

Adequately checked had meant they've broken the

Time sequence set back a thousand years into

Our past or their future, making us none existent.

As I stepped toward the platform I heard the sound

Of the doors turning I went toward the exit upon the other side.

Coming in from there too, I was trapped and now I knew,

I was tracked by infrared scanners as they were only toying with me.

While keeping me in one of their ingenious creations,

A super charged electro volt cage while they repair

The alteration room, not knowing what was next to come,

And why they didn't destroy me, I didn't know yet remembering,

My thoughts well thinking about the time displacer and how

They can change everything or create a paradox if their

Not careful. Also, thinking if one of us can go back though it's

Risky. It's all that's left.

Now, having both Matrixes they combined the power.

After an exchange for the code they subliminally revived

From my memory which I let them blocking out my inner

Memory banks so they wouldn't happen to find the location

Of our third base The Orbital. The code opened the Matrix container,

Which I don't remember placing it there. They released what was

Left of our men whom they've captured by doing this I had

To dump my inner core at the same time going through their

Computer files to find their weaknesses which I could not

Possibly decode myself but I stored this information.

And now allowing my own people to think I betray them.

For they knew with both Matrixes they could easily recapture

Them and find the coordinates of The Orbital on their own.

Chapter 4: The Dream State

Unknowing his subconscious takes control of his conscious mind.

At times because of in the past he was hypnotically under rooted

Of his own past as were all others of his kind.

From this transfer he underwent left a gap in his subconscious to conscious

Not knowing time lapses he goes into a sort of trance.

Allowing his interfacing and sociopathic to interlog.

Meaning he has the total capacity and unwillingness to undergo

Certain acts to complete his mission as to his subconscious knows

About the time rupture from the past he lived and survived

Through. So forth he is wrapped into the time dis-reference,

Making him uncontrollably caught in his own destiny which the

Past, present, and future complete the time line or time lines.

But the space and time continual's never changing course may soon

Be as we say brought to a halt forever, creating a vortex, undoubtedly

Destroying our dimension. To survive he must create an alternate

Dimension which we're most likely living in now, completing one

Part of a process which will go on for eternity.

You see we are in a never ending race to complete

Our eternity by doing this we must fight for our own

Future, by beating them in all technologies until we complete

The time displacer and create our world over so they can do

This again and again. If they reach this point in time before us

It will break a chain that's been linked together for eternity

And shall be for another. This is our secret to be kept for

Eternity in a zone we're welcomed to for no other race would

Dare tamper with Zone X.

Alone we watch the stars and alone we'll be.

As I've seen the future and I've seen the past.

And I've seen your lives fade just as fast.

For I'm your guide upon this trip. You've seen me now

And you'll see me again. Now, listen to my rhyme.

All you children who dream into the future,

I implore you don't fuck with time!

Though we may already be locked into our own time wave

Of never ending-ness, we may persist into this eternal hell.

For I know my name and you shall learn it as I am immortal.

I live eternity and you live just but death. For I've been

Plagued to this curse by theirs and my own hand. Forgiving

Myself as I'm in hell keeping you alive eternal. Being now,

As you shall know my hell as it becomes yours alone. While

I crush your mind with insanity as I flick the switch of

Life and death reliving all your pain and sorrow. As every time

You see someone die, I've thrown that switch. Though you think

Their dead, their just reliving their life again; same form,

Same identity, same mind, same life, as they watch you die again,

And reborn again in an alternate dimension. Now, feel my vengeance

As my wrath creeps upon you as I write this again and again.

For I have another dark secret to reveal. Now, have patience

As I slip back into this tale.

I as a young boy, would lay upon my back

Thinking of death and its limits and advantages.

And I thought it's simple to die but it's so hard to live.

As I did not want to die, though at times I just wished I could

Disappear from reality. Then I thought there is no reality.

This is but a dream I shall never awake from or shall you.

Deep in thought I wondered where our soul came from. It came

From nowhere, it was already here and always will be here

Caught amongst eternity with no way to escape and nowhere to

Escape to.

Around me the world grew dark as I created my own world inside.

But well aware of my immediate surroundings, strange and weird

Happenings would occur while I looked upon the mirror of life.

As it fogged and turned to an icy mist, I could see visions

Of light and dark and visions of the future and the past. And the

Future that had past and the past that became the future, including

The present of the future past.

I became time and you became lost.

I filled with power as you weakened.

Knowing all I became the mirror of death.

Facing god I ignited the twilight above.

Upon my knees, he said rise my son, I am you

And you are me. As I turned I knew that face,

It was my own reflection. Then he said,

The world is yours and the world is mine,

And then he said, take my world and I'll

Take your world. Then with my hands upon the mirror

As his were meeting, I say, my world is yours and yours mine.

Within no time barrier, I crossed this dimension.

Time had stopped, then he said in his time, you fool,

With a laughing cry, Welcome To Zone X!

In my anger, I smashed the mirror, hurling me forever into hell.

As I looked around I saw the chaos I brought about.

For I was not alone, I doomed them all to hell. So I looked

Into the future as man forgot the past, as I looked, there was

No past that which we pave the future and try to dig up the past.

Chapter 6: A Fresh Start

Now, as I opened my eyes, being removed from the separation chamber.

Knowing only the Controller Alliance they armed me with their weapons

Of mass destruction and giving me my commands to go back into time

And reach the point of intersection and destroy the one who was sent

Back to open the new dimension which we arose from creating eternal

Control for the Controllers or destroying our dimension by him not

Returning. It's a chance they're willing to take.

Alone I reappeared in a familiar place which I seen millions of people

In a suspended state of animation which seemed to be under ground, not

Remembering my past. This I did not understand as the walls were lined

With SSA chambers and each one filled with a single personnel as I walked

Down these halls it dawned on me. I've been here before now, going through

The computer files realizing we had a nuclear war and these are the survivors

And this is but one of the facilities around the world. Going through the

Computer code ID recognizing my pattern. Puzzled, I looked back at a flashing

Light.

And there it was, his time hole appeared.

It was then I released the mass destruction weapon with three

Minutes and counting as then the computer analogued my presence and

There it was, the Matrix of Life and Death combined as one. Picking

It up I looked it was him as it was me. I started to lose control

Of my functions, dropping the Matrix as it split I stumbled for my

Gate as it reappeared as he stumbled for his. He seemed to fade to

Nothingness as I dove into my gate.

Now, I am alive. It seemed I slept a thousand years in this suspension

Capsule. Now, I will live again and soon to be metal as I always said,

Immortality is immense.

While looking around, thinking why was I the only one awakened. Walking

Toward the console I saw a flashing light as I saw another moving fast

As I seen him pick up half the Matrix, while carrying a girl on his shoulder,

Then disappear back into the light.

Where he came from or where he was going or who he or she was

And soon the console went up in flames. The suspension chambers started

Bursting as I saw the other half of the Matrix. The walls started shaking,

Altering the molecular structure of everything around me. Grabbing hold

Of the Matrix, I ran toward the other flashing light. Not knowing what would

Happen when I stepped into it. Looking back around me, I saw it start to

Fade so I said, fuck it and jumped into it as it kind of went super nova

Around me.

They merged, each dimension changing, becoming one, breaking the endless

Chain that kept us caught in hell for eternity. Our time travel wasn't

Over yet, for we shall never know what may destroy us? For all we know,

We just about created a potential paradox.

Now, you have to understand this could very well be happening as I speak.

In my world and your each dimension continually merging caught into

An even worse S.T.C. until it's been altered somehow or forever collapsing

Into each other, shrinking the fabric of the universe until the mass density

Ration of space and time becomes so dense between each unit of space and time,

Eventually creating another so-called big bang. Evolving into the ultimate

S.T.C. by forming life again and again over a period of zillions of years,

Until the process starts all over, making us caught in an immortal prison,

Bringing a new meaning to space and time. For we are in a world of shit!

Suddenly, I came through the other side. I was half man, half machine.

Carrying the girl I longingly miss and truly love. Strangely it all

Came back to me and made sense. For I am him and he is me. Knowing things

To the last details as though they seem as but dreams, as the world had

Changed and so did I.

Helping us through, as he called me commander and said, your new quarters

Are arranged and you will be returning to the Earth Base as to the Wasteland,

For the briefing and further training for our encounter with the Controller

Network within two hours.

Now, in our quarters, trying to gently wake her with a kiss.

As my madness surged at the beauty I held before me. As I called her

By name, Rena. As she looked up at me and said with the softest voice,

My young love, you don't have to understand as long as we're together as

Though we both felt the passion between us, dimming the light.

Chapter 6: The Awakening

Aboard my craft I looked back at The Orbital,

As it just melted into the background of the dark space.

Appearing to be just another star in the heavens,

As I thought anything is quite possible in a realm

With such vast dimensions, that are unexplored.

And others that we'll never find as some we may

Be utterly cast into for eternity. And others we'll

Find by our own mistakes without searching for them.

We become entrapped in them as though we're not already

Caught among them from the start.

Now, as I look ahead seeing a lifeless planet stricken

By men whom don't exist in my eyes, men whom plagues themselves

To this hell and all others to come while our leaders foiled among

Their powers. We tried to engage ourselves in the matter of our

Future, never to think of the horror that would succumb us.

For we knew what was happening. We did not have the ability to maintain

Control once the world had been obliterated by our hands.

Falling to pieces, the mutants ravaged the lands and brought about

Total and complete anarchy. At this time, the surviving engineers forged

The Matrix of Life and Death, which made time travel possible as the

High command planned out the inevitability of our own end.

Seeing here they planned to change the past erasing the past thousand

Years of terror, proving a theory of time to an extent, you can't change

The past without changing the future or as I spell it out to you, time

Has conquered man.

Upon The Planetary Base, I seen as twenty legions greeted me

As I arrived looking on in the thermal heat. They stood tall

And proud, gazing about I saw in the distance the ruins of what

Was known as a city. And in its day it was high and mighty, as the

People roamed freely, going about their business the desert almost,

Swallowed its existence while the heat rising fogged my vision.

As these are the sands of doom which shall embrace us all in our

Own civilizations, as we know them to fall.

And beyond the ice slowly melts, from the glaciers of the last and man

Made ice age, which imposed upon us surely devastated our existence.

And wondering how such creatures so called mutants survived this plague

And so forth the other which killed many and transformed them. As we all

Know the mentor which wandered our world and now rests somewhere lurking

In the shadows, as it sleeps patiently waiting to be awaken. For his name is radition!

So forth, our meeting had adjourned as we planned our final attack sequence.

As we engage into eternal and mortal attack simulation status upon earth.

In the wastelands we trained for battle to avenge our proceeding processors.

And soon we shall engage in the world of death and destruction, emerging one

Armada. For the victory lance has been hurled. We shall know not fear or pain,

Nor death as we dive through the middle of hell and all the world is doomed

To despair. Forever, we'll move forward in this time hole which consumes our

Very being. As the world goes backwards and our minds are erased by time. And

Madness strikes all who live this life and sees this black cloud which

Settles upon our ever existence.

Time hole apparent, approaching interception.

Ten seconds and closing, time quake recognition.

Time seizure-glitch at standing notice.

Elapsed time two seconds, immediate warning.

From the dust and rubble emerged their armada,

With the sudden after shock from this time shift.

Space and time speed up, by this hole in the fabric of the universe.

As it gorws, alternate dimensions will be undoubtedly sucked together

At different points in time, an uncontrollable time rift made by our own

Hands. And now, another great war has begun in the space age of A. L.

Two hundred light years away, a very different quasar now discovered NGC-1275.

And this is no ordinary quasar. From earth you see it as a normal star

In your backyard telescopes, but this great engine at work is sucking

The very fabric of the universe out of existence. For at the center of

It is so powerful, no man made ship may cross its boundaries. Located there

Is something known to be Object X. This is the center of all space. This is

The center of all time. This is the center of all life and death. And now it

Is the center of Zone X.

This is no star, as many galaxies are devoured into its very being.
It spreads fear and doom as here an old enemy awakens. And he is god,
As he who is radiation plunders all as it spreads from him like a
Plague of an unseen dark shadow. As the jets of hell protrude ever closer
To our universe, like an arm to catch with and feed himself. As the energy
Released, is just as much as is taken in. For it is known as a black hole
Of complete and utter death. And there is no way to stop its movement. It's
Uncontrollably out of our hands. And when we're gone, others will feat it,
As it feeds again until the mass density ratio is so tight, as I ask a
Question. As the pressure of space declines and the tremendous pressure
Builds up inside this great device of its unknown endless depths and who
Knows what's beyond space, will it implode as another dimension crashes
Through ours or will it explode, creating that inevitable big bang again?
Is it the end or just a new beginning?

Upon The Orbital, the rift had emerged sleeping hunters,

As they planned their acts interstellarly with High Controller

Command. Their orders were to capture the female lover of Commander T-Sun,

Which was named Rena. Planned out as they say, to the T, they captured her

Ship and became those who were already aboard it.

And now being proclaimed the royal princess, but not officially yet.

She was supposed to board the cruiser for a safe return to earth

With her eternally loyal guardians. They would fight to their death

Protecting her life. Orders from the Commander which to them is a

Privilege to serve the ordinance of The Survivor Alliance.

Bombarding the Planetary Base with their full potential

Of unlimited fire power, strangely.

Now, as I merge with the DLM for battle I await to be released from

These shackles, to complete my eternal quest, foretold the mightiest cliché

Ever fought in this time sequence. For now I am one with the Matrix,

And soon with all.

Boarding our lead cruiser, we'll launch our attacks from here.

Though our plan was defiled by a sudden time shift, we'll have to

Improvise. Reaching the outer orbit of earth, we watched the battle

From here. Trembling from within, I thought as an image appeared

Before me, has this happened before? In my sights, I concealed

The very thought that this could very well happen again.

Chapter 7: The Departure

After hours of extensive defeats and withdraws, slowly we push them back
Into the cosmos. We're sustaining great losses. Our second wave of Lunar
And Orbital Forces will soon commence. Commander, Ground Base sends that
The Princess has arrived safely, but Doctor Stone says, she's ill and she
Asks for your presence. Lieutenant, you have command. I'm going in.
Transportation will be completed in 5.6 minutes. Lieutenant Brae, sir
Make your decisions accurately and accordingly, and confer with the Fleet.
I'll be back soon enough.

Commander, Doctor walking down the corridor. He expresses his emotion with
A fearsome glimpse of love in his eye. He starts to speak, Doc! She's doing
Fine. I gave her a mild sedative. I figured she should be the one to tell
You, but she told me you wouldn't have enough time, though she should be
Coming around soon. What is it? Okay, Commander T-Sun, you're going to be a
Father. Rena is seven to eight weeks pregnant. I'm going to be a father?
He seemed almost amazed, in a state of shock.

Commander! Commander! Like he was in a trance. Commander! Oh yes. Are you

Alright? Yeah, I'm fine. I just wanna know how she is? Can I see her?

Sure, in just a minute. I'd like to see you in my office, to talk to you

About her condition. I thought you said, she was fine?

She is fine. Can't you see my condition? Tearing off her uniform as it

Fell to the floor, she takes hold of him and starts kissing him. Before he

Gets a word in edge wise.

Doctor Stone, I have my priorities and dignity. And I am a great man of
Stature. And I would not condemn myself to this unworthy and unvirtuous
Act, to this unbarring sexual retention, even though you are quite
Beautiful. I do love my lovely Princess Rena and I could not face her
Or my people if I did other wise and the mere thought of or elaboration
Of her especially and my people, just leaves my mind a blank. What would
They think of me then, even though this is hardly the right time? I think
I'd better check on her with a last glance and sigh of explanation.
He walked toward her room.

Now, once again, I gently awaken her as I call her name. Rena! She awakes.
Is that you T-Sun? With a sweet voice, she says yeah baby, it's me.
Then die! With a deep voice she spoke, pulling a laser gun out and firing
It at me as I ducked and jumped from the bed. Surprised, as two more shots
Came from the closet, hitting her three Hunters, as I was scared for Rena.
Turning towards the door, it was Stone, as naked as ever, standing there with
A laser aimed at me. I said, Doc., what's going on? What are you doing?
I'm going to take you on a journey, a ride you'll never forget.
In a louder voice, she said, I'm going to fuck you to death!

Putting her hand out to grab me, I said, well, well, well, I never thought

I'd see the day. I'd love to stay and party, but I got to go see-ya.

Go to hell bitch, as powerful light shot from the Matrix, which is merged

Into my uniform and part of my chest. I blasted her to kingdom come,

And with a quick turn, I took out the other two with my hand laser.

As I looked at the Doc., well what was supposed to be the Doc. And Rena,

I thought where in the hell have they taken her? That's it, where in hell?

We're already there as I thought, my god, Hunters. I don't believe anyone

Ever had an encounter with them before. Someone must have, their existence

Is well known. Calling for security, still thinking and looking down

At the Doc., I thought, what a waste. Then it glitched and spoke, T-Sun, you're

Existence will never ever see the female, Rena again, in this time zone. And with

An evil laugh, it laughed until it shorted out and I let out a screaming cry,

That could wake the dead's ancestors.

Now, always guarded by security, we transported up. It took almost 10.5

Minutes. They were getting closer to the main output of their inner

Space defenses. They were starting to see ships, they've never seen before.

And strange and weird weapons, and battle craft that couldn't be destroyed.

We were losing more and more, another twenty minutes and the entire first

Wave will be destroyed or completely knocked out.

Lieutenant, sir what's our current status. First of all sir, our scanners

Have picked up a large mass of energy, like a shield around the black hole.

Yeah, but that's normal. No sir, we have singled out three large bodies,

Lying unmaterialized inside of it, possibly their base sir. Yeah, possibly.

Keep scanning that area. Anything else Brae? Yes sir, second attack wave

Ready for your command. Good, we're right on schedule. Second, onward and attack.

Victory is ours or is it not? May it be time or is it not, no one ever

Thought it would stop. Is it there or is it not, as reality slips in and out.

As the time shifts steadily leave, their dread behind them or in front

Of them. Maybe, even all around them. What's reality and what's not?

And I thinking, how to stop them. Realizing no ship can enter the black hole

Without being destroyed and we assume their base lies unmaterialized inside

Of it. I thought, rematerialize it, will blow their base or bases into atoms.

Chapter 8: The Final Stage

Alert the fleet, we must find her.

Right away sir. And Brea, tell them no mercy.

We will get her back at all costs and if they hear or find anything,

Have them inform me immediately. Yes sir.

Sir, their lead ship is in sight.

All weapons at my command. Engage upon it.

And with a deep breath and a nod from his head,

He says, commence firing with an explosive exchange of fire power

Onto each other, bombarding their lead ship with ours and our other

Fleets moving in from the other bases.

The second wave will lead a slow and steady attack leading many to their

Doom. Soon their fleets will begin to take heavy loses as they get closer

And closer to this black hole. The center of their power as dimensions collide,

And all hell breaks loose. Then suddenly there are two or more of everything

Or everyone.

Sustaining a great amount of damage ourselves

And their ship drifting dead like a ghost ship, we rendered it.

I'll take a dozen elite guard and my personal guard to board their ship.
That makes fifteen. No sir, sixteen. I'm coming sir, said with a deep

Pride and dedication to me and his people.

Brae, I'd like you to stay and take command of the fleets.

Sir, of this day and age, you can trust no one or call them your friend.

As if there ever was any trust in the world. You can trust no one, not

Even yourself, but if I were to trust someone, it would be someone like you.

I think of you as a brother and friend. And I'd like to be by your side,

During combat and anywhere else, no matter what happens.

I didn't know I had any friends, let alone a brother.

Thinking to himself, I shouldn't do this, but what's the difference anymore.

I know we won't be returning. It's a fight to the death. Here or in there,

It's the same as hell and we're willing to go deeper in. We're all mad!

There's no right way and no way to solve this. It is the end.

With a brief pause from the Commander, then said, Brae, suit up. Yes sir!

Nelson, you're in command. I expect you will fulfill your duties

To us and your people? And never to retreat under no circumstances, until we

Complete our missions. If we don't return, we're all expected to die for our

Cause. We'll die anyway, if we lose. For there is nowhere left to hide,

Nowhere to escape to. Do you understand? If we don't complete this task,

We are all finished!

Now, boarding their ship. It's cold and no life supports, no power, no nothing,
Except for the transporter. Enough energy for us to transport to their
Base with no way to return and them not knowing, the self-destruct sequence
Was locked in. And when they transport, the ship will go up in a ball of
Flames, a soundless explosion. There's no sound in space except for space
Itself and up it went as they transported to their base, where they fled
Themselves.

Arriving there, we had a fine welcoming party. There were guards everywhere.
Fighting our way through, realizing that the technologies applied were
So beyond belief and the Controllers could never do this on their own.
They must be at alliance with another, an alien race. A race not knowing
What hell they've entered. Though we knew, the battle was over, right then and
There. When we discovered this I thought, we must continue and fulfill our
Secret end to this hell. Our plan will leave us alive, but at peace forever.
The plan was to destroy the time displacer inside the black hole, by
Materializing the bases, blowing space and time into infinity, for a fragment
Of a second. Leaving a plain hole in space and time, where it stopped for
A point and started back up, but all different and peaceful, knocking us back
In our own reality, our realm, the way it was and will be, hopefully.

Onward, we moved quickly.

They were closing in on us as there were more and more X-men,

Around us as they were moleculating from the walls. All matter

Seemed to be self-destructing as they had used their devices to reconstruct

Themselves from the walls, as they had hand weapons to do the same,

Using these weapons on us, hitting Brower and Tomson.

 Their suits of armored uniforms just molecularized right to their flesh,

As their flesh was no more. Stretching out from inside, they cried out.

Their skulls popped out from within and as they were dead.

A cross between skeleton and metal, coming toward us, grabbing hold of us.

From behind, picking up some of their weapons and used them back upon them.

They were an even worse sight to see, more horrifying than ever, as their

Necks grew long, as their skulls jiggled at the ends and their hands and

Feet did the same, as all their blood was flushed out, their mouths upon us,

As the scream they made was unbearable.

I gave the word to split up. It was like, every man for themselves.

The walls seemed like they were melting from the shots, intended for us.

Hitting the walls instead, as some of us were being sucked through the floor.

It was a blood bath all around and everything seeped into darkness.

All hope seemed to be lost.

Then suddenly, some of us broke through.

It was I, Brae and a few others. It was an open room and there it was,

The Time Displacer. I looked again, it was her, lying on what seemed

To be nothing but air, gravity free. There's no air here.

She was unconscious. I started to step toward her.

Then he stepped out of nowhere. It was me again, as it was I.

Commander, it's you. Yes, Lieutenant, it is. But he's from a different dimension.

It's not the real me!

I've been waiting for you. I've always been waiting for you!

In your dreams and in your nightmares, in you T-Sun!

As I am you, the product of no return.

Your world is at its end and mine. Just about to begin.

We could have destroyed you, but we needed you,

To complete the final stage.

And you did it without even knowing.

You destroyed your world and you did it with your own hand.

Now, I will be you, as I am you.

And destroy what's left of your punt dimension.

Not if I can help it and at the same time an echo that would wake time itself,

To watch, but he already is, as they said (Merge!).

Instantaneously, complete fifteen foot metal structures materialized

From the Matrix's to complete the LFM and the DLM.

But remember, only one Matrix was ever made half-light and half dark,

Half-life and half death. Now, locked in a battle to the death!

The others trying to get to the Princess, as there was a shield

Around her, as they learned, when Hanner stepped toward her

And was disintegrated almost instantly.

Firing back and forth, they blasted each other.

When out of nowhere, the LFM boosted a Matrix shot right into the DLM,

Knocking him clear across east bumblefuck, as the LFM, right on

His ass, short circuiting, the LFM went on reserve power. The DLM

Picked him up, clear over his head and bounced him off the side of the

Time Displacer, as the DLM went toward him, the LFM kicked him off his

Feet, from the floor with a powerful foot weapon, that sort of paralyzes

For a brief period and at the same time, sucks the power out of him.

Now, as the DLM lies shaking like convulsions, with electricity jumping

In and out of him, the LFM shoots the last of his booster rockets into him

And turned toward the girl, as the paralyzer wore off, he lifted his arms

And shot all six of his booster rockets into the LFM's back, completely

Penetrating the shield and blasting right through him, killing the X-Man

Inside, which seemed to be T-Sun. As it lies on the floor, you can hear

Failure, failure, override human android X-Man.

Back up procedures, deleting structure, failure, must de-merge,

Need a new host. Struggling to get up, the Matrix made an emergency

Weapon, a ball of light and the LFM threw it at the DLM, impacting into

Him, knocking out all control as he went skidding across the floor,

Then flying upward and swinging around with sparks and light and boom,

Into the wall, left him all mangled and twisted and half dead or half alive.

As the LFM barely made it on its feet, he stumbled to the girl, as Brae

Starts shouting, don't fire, you might hit her, as he picked her up, they

Thought, there's nothing we can do. Going towards the Time Displacer, then

Smashing the controls and diving through, just as another came through.

And again it looked like T-Sun, as he yelled out Ahhh, and covering his

Face, as the LFM smashes right through him, knocking all three of them

Somewhere in time forever.

Chapter 9: The Last Encounter

Commander, Commander!

Speaking with an almost dying voice, Brae!

Did we save her?

Sir, he took her through the Time Displacer.

There was nothing we could do.

Noooo! I'm going after her, (Demerge).

What time did he go to? That's the thing sir, he smashed it.

It still works, but you'll never know where they went.

I'm going through anyway. No sir! Holding me back, the three of them,

Brae, Crane, Dillan, as Brae said, we will find her again sometime

And destroy that thing. But now we must complete our task

And save our people. You're right Brae, we will find them another time.

Saying this with the solemn stare in his eyes.

Men, let's go, we have a mission to finish.

Going through the mirror gate to the Center Base,

Seeing the battle I just had and him take her

Through the Time Displacer again.

Then watching ourselves walk through the mirror gate,

As if they didn't see us, we were invisible or they were an illusion,

Or our dimensions just crossed together.

We followed them straight through again,

Not knowing what's reality or what's real anymore.

There it seemed we were in an alien world.

A bluish, whitish, glow from all seemed to be a garden of eden,

Like a heaven and there I looked down and saw on both sides,

What appeared to be a bluish water and bluish pathway.

And upon her knees I saw her as I ran toward her. They

Could not hold me back as I cried out her name, Rena!

She looked up with beauty and smiled at me, standing and reaching out

Her arms to hold me as I put my arms around her. They past right through

Her as she disappeared. Falling to my knees and looking down with tears

Rolling down my face as I thought, did she ever exist? She disappeared from

My life and so did all as the darkness was so thick, I could not see or hear

A thing. I couldn't tell if I was dead of not.

Then suddenly, a door started to open.

We were blinded by the light.

The huge door had open and there stood as far as the eye can see,

LFM's programmed to destroy us, for they must have a duplicator.

They were not merged with no man, but aliens,

Before us, what horror. They are indescribable.

They started firing upon us

And marching toward us. We fired back,

And retreated through the mirror gate.

They always said curiosity killed the cat, not humans.

Our exploring days are over. There were more and more around us.

We got to the materializer, located near the time displacer.

But as many being devastated, I hit the first switch

And told them to go through the time displacer.

As Dillan was carrying Crane and Brae's waiting for me,

I said, go, that's an order. As Brae said, we'll meet again to finish our quest.

As they jumped through I hit the second switch,

A sort of skylight opened as I could see the bases start materializing.

I looked at the heavens, as there were no heavens just flashes and glimpses

Of a never ending battle.

And then I thought with my own hands, I will now stop

It. As I saw nothing but death, sucking all to doom.

As there was no universe left, all but as white light.

I looked at them getting closer to me, then looked up

And back at them, firing at me. Now, with flames coming from

My armored suit, from their attack, I threw that last switch.

And with a laughing cry I said, you fools, welcome to Zone X!

Diving through the time displacer, instantaneously materializing

Completely, all three Vortex Bases, dissolving all space and time.

All matter itself, in one flash, erasing centuries of death and destruction

Of the past, present, future, and the future to come.

For there is a whole new world out there.

The world is cruel as the day never ends.

Only halted for a brief period as night passes by.

Time is what they said, time, they came forth to me,

From beyond, only to give me a piece of this time.

Who knows, not even time, for a piece of time could

Last as long as I want it to last. So, I used it sparingly

And enjoyed my life, even though hell was enjoyment in this world.

For we know no other and I used it to the best of my knowledge.

All things and all life is time and I own a piece of it and to make

It last as long as I want and so do you, under total prosperity.

The sun is lit with a great light from within myself, so join my quest,

Which you're already living. But all knowing this life is the journey.

The journey you will for take with or without my help. I tell you, the quest

Will never end, then this tale will never end. Lost in time forever,

The unknown, no point, no guilt, no worry, or absolute, shall I say, time

Could be your friend or it could be your worst enemy to boot.

Welcome To Zone X   89-91

Written by I who wrote The Quest

And others before, and others to come.

Ignorance is of men, whom shouldn't live.

Listen now, listen again to what I say.

Your grievance is only to lose,

Fuck them, take out a gun and shoot.